THE RUNAWAY AVOCADO

By:

Rhea G. Madison James

ISBN: 978-1-63945-247-7 (Paperback)
        978-1-63945-248-4 (Ebook)

Writers' Branding
1800-608-6550
www.writersbranding.com
orders@writersbranding.com

One day, a man named Mr. Chris was picking avocados outside in his backyard.

Author Rhea G. Madison James

Mr. Chris loves avocados. He picks them for his world's famous guacamole that he serves in his restaurant.

On the tree, there were many ripe avocados. Mr. Chris picked a lot yesterday. A little later, one of the avocados disappeared. Mr. Chris was looking up, looking down, and looking all around. He seemed to think the avocado jumped out of the basket and ran as fast as he could. It took a while for Mr. Chris to notice that the Avocado Man was running down the hill.

The Avocado Man said, "Away I go, so please don't follow."

Mr. Chris started to run after the Avocado Man and the Avocado Man said "Run, run, as fast as you can cause you will not catch me to make guacamole with your quick little hands." Suddenly, the Avocado Man ran as fast as a cheetah.

Author Rhea G. Madison James

The Avocado Man ran until he approached a building that was government property. He entered inside and looked up, looked down, and looked all around.

As the Avocado Man entered the building, the Watermelon Man was at the front desk. The Avocado Man asked the Watermelon Man if he can help him.

The Avocado Man explained he was so scared that he ran as fast as he could. He did not want Mr. Chris to catch him, so he could make guacamole with his quick little hands. The Watermelon Man said, "This is the Governor and Lieutenant Governor's Office. I can give you a mask and no one will notice you."

The Avocado Man started speaking in Spanish. *"¿Que día es hoy?"* The Watermelon Man asked, "What are you saying?" The Lieutenant Governor was passing and said, "He was asking what is today's date?" The Watermelon Man was so confused.

Soon after the governor was leaving the building, the Avocado Man said, *"¿Buenos días, que pasa?"* The governor said, "Good morning I am well, and you are?" The governor's phone rang, and he left. The Watermelon Man was so happy because he did not know what to say.

Mr. Chris was outside at the front door. As the governor was leaving, he said, "If you don't have a mask no service."

Mr. Chris said, "Sir I have no mask." Can you help me?

The governor said, "I will call someone don't you worry even though I'm in a hurry."

Mr. Chris said, "Thank you, thank you."

The Avocado Man was hiding, gliding, and sliding. How funny!

Hiding

Gliding

Sliding

Author Rhea G. Madison James

The Watermelon Man gave Mr. Chris a mask and asked, "How may I help you?"

Mr. Chris said, "I am looking for an Avocado Man. He ran, ran as fast as he could because he did not want me to catch him with my quick little hands."

The Watermelon Man did not have a chance to answer.

Author Rhea G. Madison James

The Avocado Man slid right out and yelled, "Oh no! Please do not catch me with your quick little hands! Correrá, correrá tan rapido como pueda."

The Watermelon asked, "What are you saying?"

Mr. Chris said, "He is saying he will run, run as fast as he can."

Mr. Avocado Man dashed, then crashed.

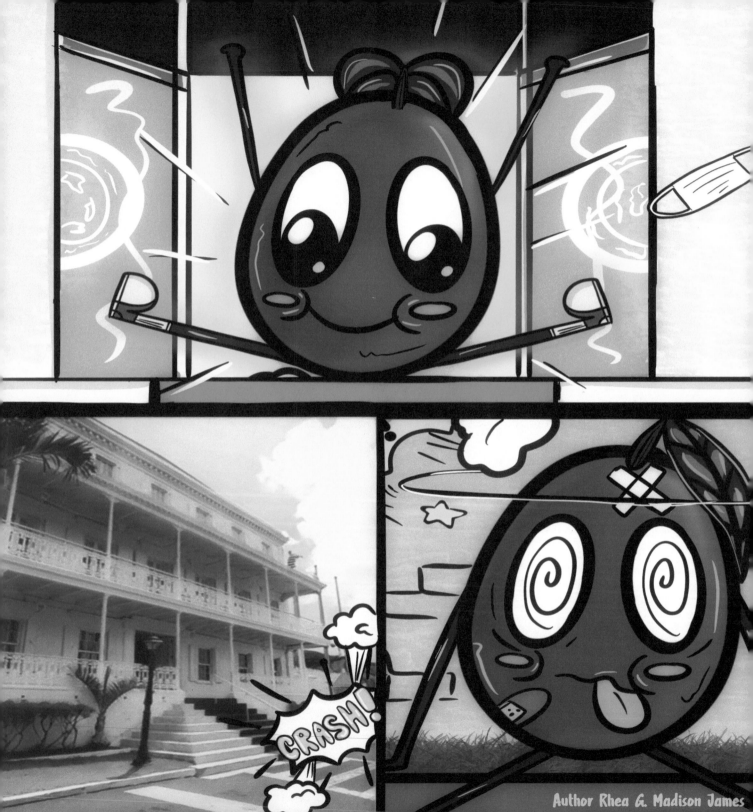

CRASH!

Author Rhea G. Madison James

The Watermelon Man said to the Avocado Man, "Take it easy before you get queasy."

They started talking while walking. Mr. Chris decided not to take the Avocado Man and make his famous guacamole however they all went across the street to have some tasty lemonade.

Author Rhea G. Madison James

They all laughed and enjoyed each other's company while relaxing on the reclining chairs.

No more run, run, as fast as you can because we now have each other to love as one fam.

The End

Author Rhea G. Madison James

About the Author

My name is **Rhea G. Madison James**. I am a 10-year-old student living in the beautiful island of St. Thomas, United States Virgin Islands. I attend the Virgin Islands Montessori School and Peter Gruber International Academy on St. Thomas, USVI. I have one sibling named Ricky James Jr. I enjoy dancing, karate, tennis, and writing. I love to give and believe everyone should treat people the way they want to be treated.

About the Illustrator

Deja-Marie Simon is an 18-year-old, high school graduate from the Virgin Islands Montessori School and Peter Gruber International Academy on St. Thomas, USVI. She enjoys drawing, painting, and digital art. Deja-Marie attends Pratt Institute of Art University in Brooklyn, New York majoring in 2D Animation and Digital Arts.

Beautiful St. Thomas, U.S. Virgin Islands

Magen's Bay Beach in St. Thomas, U.S. Virgin Islands

CPSIA information can be obtained
at www.ICGtesting.com
Printed in the USA
BVHW051600211221
624594BV00002B/85

* 9 7 8 1 6 3 9 4 5 2 4 7 7 *